PICTURE BOOK STUDIO USA

ERMANNO CRISTINI
LUIGI PURICELLI
IN MY GARDEN

As I wander through my garden on a clear and sunny day,
I meet many friends: my cat, who is looking for mice; the hen,
who searches for food; the white rabbits in their hutch,
and many more . . .

I have painted them all for you on the following pages. There is
so much to discover in every garden; keep your eyes open,
observe carefully, and have a little patience. Then all our little
friends will appear – even the nimble lizard, the colorful butterfly,
and the red lady bug with its black spots. But there are
still more . . .

How many creatures can you find? Look carefully, some of them
are hiding in their surroundings. Can you name them all? Or can
you make up a story to go with the pictures?

1. grass
2. wall lizard
3. clover
4. housefly
5. chicken
6. earthworm
7. mole
8. cricket
9. land tortoise
10. lettuce
11. caterpillar
12. lady bug
13. looper
14. great tit
15. dandelion
16. rabbit
17. spider
18. red admiral butterfly
19. capricorn beetle
20. toad
21. hedgehog
22. praying mantis
23. milkweed bug
24. house cat
25. field mouse
26. horse

Text copyright © 1985, Neugebauer Press USA, Inc.
Published in USA by Picture Book Studio USA,
an imprint of Neugebauer Press USA, Inc.
Distributed by Alphabet Press, Natick, MA 01760.
Distributed in Canada by Vanwell Publishing, St. Catharines,
Published in U.K. by Neugebauer Press Publishing Ltd., London.

Library of Congress Cataloging in Publication Data
Cristini, Ermanno.   In my garden.
Translation of: Falter, Blumen, Tiere und ich.
Summary: Presents a wordless panorama of assorted
domestic animals sharing a garden environment with
a variety of small wild creatures.
1. Garden fauna – Pictorial works – Juvenile literature.
2. Gardens – Pictorial works – Juvenile literature.
[1. Gardens – Pictorial works. 2. Animals – Pictorial works.]
I. Puricelli, Luigi, ill. II. Title.
QL49.C7513 1985   591   85-9402
ISBN 0-88708-007-3 (pbk.)   ISBN 0-907234-05-4 (hc.)